For my husband Shawn, who never stopped encouraging me.

For Nyasia, Autumn, Jordan, and Anayah– my greatest loves & inspirations;

And for every child that has ever wondered:

May you never forget that you are fearfully and wonderfully made.

-S.F.

To my mother, Donna, who taught me faith. To Khye and Yori for being my biggest fans. To Jennifer, for keeping me covered in prayer. To Allison, for your guidance. To my family and friends for loving and supporting me without boundaries.

-S.F.

Edited by J.Carter

Illustrated by Lolacreative

Creative Design by Anayah Fleming

Sometimes I sit and wonder what people think of me.

When I walk into a crowded room, who do they really see?

Sometimes I sit and wonder,
will I make a friend today?

Will other children want to play,
or will they run away?

Sometimes I sit and wonder, as I go throughout my day.

Do people listen when I talk, do they care what I have to say?

Sometimes I sit and wonder, will they like what I am wearing?

Is the color too dull, does it fit me well, or why won't they stop staring?

Sometimes I sit and wonder, yet it's never very clear.

Maybe my curls are too tight, style– not right, or just the texture of my hair.

Sometimes I sit and wonder, even after a hundred tries.

Too big, too small, too round, too tall—is there a perfect size?

Sometimes I sit and wonder, and I'm overwhelmed by fright.

Are the other children smarter than me, will my answer be wrong or right?

Sometimes I sit and wonder longer
than I am even aware.

Will I ever walk like the other kids,
or always be in a chair?

Then one day, while I was wondering, I decided I should pray.

I began to talk to the one who created me in a very special way.

So no longer do I wonder if anyone listens when I talk at all.

I get on my knees, pray out loud, and He answers when I call.

No longer do I wonder if
they see me or just my skin.

What's important to me is
whose I am and who I am
within.

I no longer wonder if I'm special or if I'll ever make a friend.

God's spirit lives inside of me, and He'll be there to the end.

I no longer sit and wonder if I will pass or fail *any* test.

The way I learn may be different, but I have the mind of Christ, nonetheless.

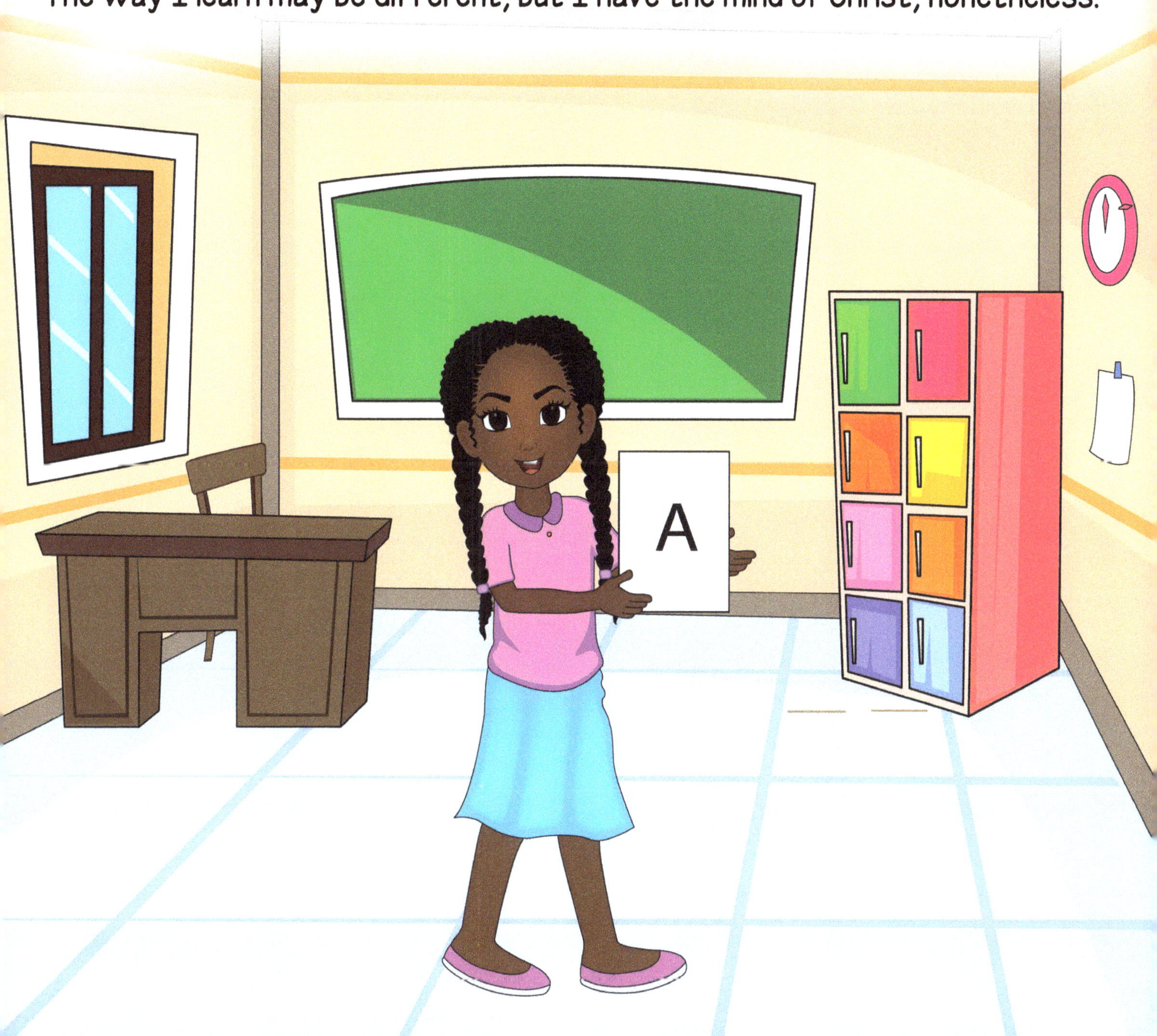

My hair is fine just the way it is, so no longer do I sit and wonder.

My texture comes from the one who fights all my battles; He's the ultimate contender.

My style, clothes, and size don't matter at all, so wondering is no longer my thing.

I'm loved by God, an heir to the throne, the daughter of a King.

So if you're wondering about all my confidence,
then I guess you will agree.

That the one who created the moon, sun, and
the stars is the one who created me.

www.ingramcontent.com/pod-product-compliance
Lightning Source LLC
Chambersburg PA
CBHW040907070726
47599CB00038B/2343